Dedicated to my daughters, Kylie and Grace! You continue to inspire me every single day. I love you and thank you for being the amazing daughters that you are. Love always and forever!

—Mommy

A Letter from the Author

Well hello, boys and girls! How are you feeling today? I hope you are feeling as wonderful as you are a human being! I am a mommy who used to be a first-grade teacher. My goal in this book is to teach you how amazing you are, starting from the inside of your body. You do know you're awesome, right?

I have two daughters, Kylie and Grace. They are both the loves of my life, as I'm sure you are to your parents. One day, Kylie and Grace had to get blood work done, which is part of their yearly wellness visit with the pediatrician. Kylie was very calm and cool about having blood taken from her tiny arm. Grace, on the other hand, was not so happy to experience this part of life. Have you ever had blood work done? I certainly have, and believe it or not, I actually think blood work is the coolest thing ever! I know that sounds crazy, but it's actually a story that tells your doctor, parents, and you about what is going on inside your beautiful self.

Sit back, relax, and enjoy this little story about your blood. Feel free to laugh, think, ask questions (when it's an appropriate time, of course), and learn about your body. Are you ready?

www.mascotbooks.com

The Story of Me from the Inside Out

For more information, please contact:
Mascot Books
620 Herndon Parkway, Suite 320
Herndon, VA 20170
info@mascotbooks.com

Library of Congress Control Number: 2021907841

CPSIA Code: PRT0421A
ISBN-13: 978-1-64543-867-0

Printed in the United States

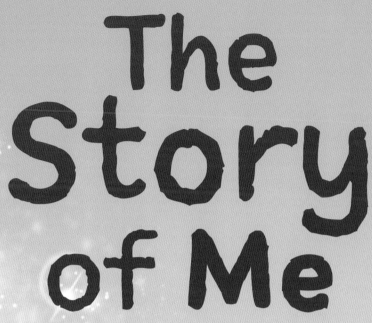

The Story of Me

from the Inside Out

Christine Heimbach

Illustrated by Nidhom

Once upon a regular day at home on a rainy summer morning, two little girls, Kylie and Grace, had to get some blood work done. Now, Kylie and Grace were sisters who were very much alike, yet also quite different. Kylie was almost a full two years older than Grace. As they clambered into their car before getting on the way to get blood taken at the lab, both girls had very different opinions and feelings about this task the doctor required from them.

Kylie said to Grace, "I don't care about this blood work. It's no big deal!"

Grace looked at her sister in complete and utter horror and disgust. She hollered, "Are you out of your ever-loving, brown-haired, silly, crazy, big sister, cuckoo bird mind? Kylie, what's wrong with you? Don't you realize that a nurse is going to suck the blood right out of us? Huh? Do ya?"

Kylie replied, "Yeah, so?"

Grace seriously thought she was losing her mind as she tried to convince her big sister how awful this was going to be!

When Kylie and Grace got to the lab where the blood would be "sucked" (according to Grace), Kylie got out of the car like a rock star. She walked up to the building like a cool, calm, little cucumber. Grace, on the other hand, could barely let her feet touch the ground. She was sweating and shaking, with her tummy grumbling, heart pounding, and knees squeezing close together. Grace looked like a wilted petunia, walking through the desert, approaching a dreaded, prickly cactus with her shoulders shrugged and arms folded.

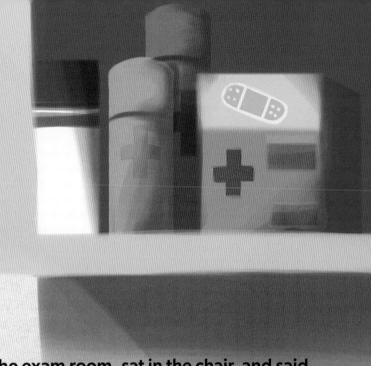

Kylie walked right into the exam room, sat in the chair, and said, "Mom, I got this. I don't need your help!"

Her mom said, "Well, alrighty then, but I'll be right here if you want to hold my hand!"

Kylie stayed relaxed, watching the needle as it entered her delicate skin, and then as it was pulled out gently. She even got to choose her own cartoon bandage.

"Cool!" she said as she hopped out of the chair.

G race, on the other hand, was dripping with sweat! She could barely hold herself up in the chair, even with her mommy sitting behind her, cradling her. As the nurse walked toward Grace, she saw what she imagined was a monster just ready to suck her blood out!

Grace started to cry tears of worry and fear. The nurse gently inserted the needle and started to draw Grace's blood. Grace became white as a cotton ball. Her tummy started to hurt and she couldn't see anything. The nurse quickly put her on the exam table to lie down, gave her some ice for her head, and a cool drink of water. It took about five minutes or so for Grace's skin color to return.

When they were all finished, everyone got back into the car to talk about the experience. As the girls compared their bandages, they didn't notice that their mom had turned toward their favorite diner.

Grace asked her big, brave sister what her strategy was to get through it.

Kylie smiled and said, "Oh, it's easy! Just imagine there is a beautiful bouquet of flowers in front of you. Then, you slowly breathe in the smell of the pretty flowers and hold it in your nose and imagination for a few seconds. When you breathe out, Grace, make sure to do it slowly like you are blowing out a candle."

"Even though this was tough, you did such a great job!" Kylie concluded.

"Yeah, I had to get through it so mom could take us for a special breakfast of pancakes, bacon, and orange juice afterward!"

Grace replied, "I kept thinking of us all sitting down to a delicious breakfast while Mommy hugged me and that's what I did to let the nurse take my blood."

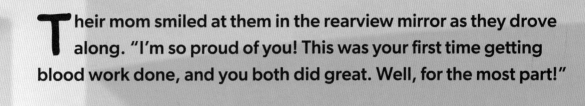

Their mom smiled at them in the rearview mirror as they drove along. "I'm so proud of you! This was your first time getting blood work done, and you both did great. Well, for the most part!"

She winked at both girls and said, "We were going for breakfast anyway, whether we had blood work or not!"

Did you know that your blood can actually tell a story? Seriously! Not kidding! It can tell your doctor, your parents, and you what is going on in your body. It's like there's an author living inside you, just waiting to tell this incredible story! I know that it sounds as wild as a kangaroo jumping into a swimming pool while holding an ice cream cone in both hands.

our blood

irst of all, your body can tell us what type of blood you have. You may have chocolate, vanilla, or strawberry! Just kidding! Blood types are things like A, B, AB, or O. An A doesn't mean you're doing extremely well in school—it's just the type of blood you have, and different letters mean different things! If you ever need to receive blood for surgery, the doctors know what type of blood you will need from someone who has donated. People like to help others, so many decide to donate blood. Pretty cool, huh?

Your blood tells the story of how well your heart is working, what your vitamin levels are, what your kidneys are up to these days, how your liver is behaving, how well you're eating, and so much more! Did you know that your blood can also tell the doctors if you have an infection? All of these things are like chapters in a book, and when you line them all up, you can read the whole story from start to finish!

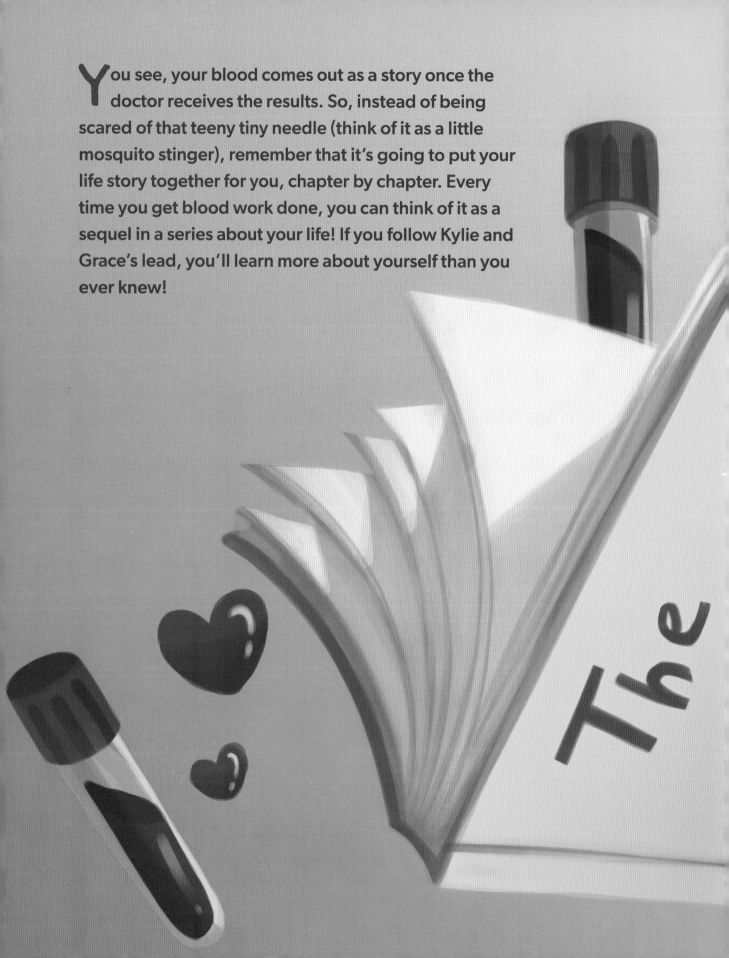

You see, your blood comes out as a story once the doctor receives the results. So, instead of being scared of that teeny tiny needle (think of it as a little mosquito stinger), remember that it's going to put your life story together for you, chapter by chapter. Every time you get blood work done, you can think of it as a sequel in a series about your life! If you follow Kylie and Grace's lead, you'll learn more about yourself than you ever knew!

About the Author

Hello, everyone! My name is **Christine Heimbach.** Now that you've learned about the story of you, here's a little bit of *my* story! I went to The College of Saint Elizabeth to earn my bachelor's and master's degrees in Elementary Education with a concentration in Special Education. I'm a former elementary teacher, and had to retire prematurely due to health issues. My passion in life was to teach children how to read, write, spell, and solve math problems, as I believe this is a foundation for the remainder of what is to come in school and in life. I'm married to the man of my dreams, and we have two beautiful daughters: Kylie and Grace. Kylie and Grace are the absolute loves of my life and are the air in my lungs. They make me so proud to be their mom. My husband, Jeff, and I are animal lovers, so we have three Rottweilers and one cat: Bella, Sophie, Lucy, and Lexi. My life is complete with my amazing husband, two incredible daughters, and our loving fur babies! I'm blessed beyond belief!